# dick bruna

# miffy
# at the
# gallery

EGMONT

I'm going, Mrs Bunny said

to see a gallery

it's full of lovely works of art,

who'd like to come with me?

I will, said Mr Bunny, but

Miffy is much too small.

Too small, said Miffy, no I'm not,

I'm really big and tall!

So Miffy was allowed to go

and off the Bunnies went,

what fun to see a gallery,

Miff wondered what it meant.

The first thing Miffy saw was this

a painting on the wall,

a nice red apple, Miffy said

and ripe enough to fall.

Look, Miffy, that's a mobile,

hanging above you there,

the shapes are hooked together

to keep them in the air.

A bear, a real bear, cried Miff.

But Father Bun said: no,

a real live bear is nice and soft,

this one is stone, you know.

That sun is blue, thought Miffy,

I'd paint a yellow one,

and yet a famous painter

painted that bright blue sun.

Those stripes are very pretty,

I like this painting too,

but should I look this way or that?

I'm not sure what to do!

Look, Miffy, said her father,

a rabbit, just like you.

Oh no, it isn't, Miffy said,

I'm real, and I'm not blue!

That one is fine, said Miffy,

the colours are so clear,

as if the artist cut them out

and stuck them over here.

Time to go home, her parents said,

and Miff said, what a shame,

I think art galleries are fun

I'm very glad we came.

And later on, when I grow up

– in just a year or two –

do you know what I really want?

to be an artist, too!

# miffy's library

miffy
miffy's dream
miffy's bicycle
miffy at the gallery
miffy at school
miffy at the playground

miffy in hospital
miffy at the zoo
miffy at the seaside
miffy the fairy
miffy's garden
miffy and the new baby

miffy is crying
miffy's birthday
miffy in the snow
miffy dances

MIX
From responsible sources
FSC® C021195
FSC www.fsc.org

"nijntje in het museum"
First published in Great Britain 1998 by Egmont UK Limited
239 Kensington High Street, London W8 6SA.
Publication licensed by Mercis Publishing bv, Amsterdam
Original text Dick Bruna © copyright Mercis Publishing bv, 1997
Illustrations Dick Bruna © copyright Mercis bv, 1997
Original English translation © copyright Patricia Crampton, 1997
The moral right of the author has been asserted.
Printed in Germany
All rights reserved
ISBN 978 1 4052 0981 6
20 19 18 17 16 15 14
34900/13